The Frightened Little Flower Bud

By Renée Paule & G R Hewitt

Cover design, artwork and all illustrations by Renée Paule and G R Hewitt

Printed in Ireland by DPS, Carrick on Shannon

www.reneepaule.com

British Spelling Version

ISBN: 978-0-9935098-3-4

The Frightened Little Flower Bud

Tragopogon Pratensis
Irish name - *Finidí na muc*

This plant is also known as 'Goat's-beard' or Jack-go-to-bed-at-noon. The plant usually closes into a bud after midday, but for the purposes of my story I made it the evening.

The root can be cooked and eaten - the flower can be added to salads.

The wind blew a gentle breeze and carried with it a tiny seed.

The tiny seed swirled in the cool breeze travelling far and wide until it landed in a pretty garden.

All through the winter months the little seed lay safely under the autumn leaves.

As winter turned to spring, the little seed germinated. Its root grew down as the stem grew up.

The root grew deeper and deeper into the soil as the stem grew taller and taller until, one day, a little flower bud appeared at the very top.

But, when it was time for
the little bud to bloom,
she became afraid ...

... for she'd heard on the wind about the sun and how it might scorch and wilt her lovely petals.

The little bud heard stories about the rain and how it might spoil her lovely and colourful petals.

She feared the wind, for it might blow her
lovely, colourful and delicate petals away.

The little bud had listened to stories about the bees and how they might sting - she became afraid of them too.

She heard that when she flowered, she'd die soon afterwards.

Sometimes the little bud peeked out at the garden, but when she saw how beautiful the other flowers were, she became afraid of something else - what if *she* wasn't as beautiful?

Every day, because the little bud listened to the stories that rode on the wind, she became more and more afraid of all the terrible things that *might* happen to her.

Outside became a scarier and scarier place for the little bud, so she kept her petals tucked safely inside.

The day came when the little bud was unable to hide anymore - it was her time to bloom - and *bloom* she did!

Her perfectly formed petals were delicate.

She was colourful!

She was beautiful!

She was *so* special!

The sun shone on the little flower and its rays were warm and soothing - they didn't scorch or wilt her petals.

She felt the wind
flutter her petals as
it passed between
them - they didn't
blow away.

When the rain fell, the little flower found it refreshing and cleansing - it didn't spoil any of her petals.

When the bees drank of her nectar, they tickled her face, but they didn't sting.

The little flower was so happy and full of joy that she no longer feared the things she heard on the wind. She never gave another thought to how beautiful she may or may not be.

In the evening, as the sun set, the little flower tucked herself up into a bud again, and fell fast asleep.

The following morning, as the clouds drifted lazily by, the little flower - feeling refreshed by the morning dew - stretched out her pretty petals.

A new day had begun.

Then, one fine morning, the little flower didn't notice that her petals had gone or that she'd become a spectacular seed clock. She didn't notice the wind picking up her seeds and carrying them into the air …

… carrying them far and wide.

One of the tiny seeds landed in a
pretty garden.

After the winter, the seed
grew and a little bud appeared
at the very top of its stem ...

… but the little flower bud became afraid of the things she could hear on the wind.

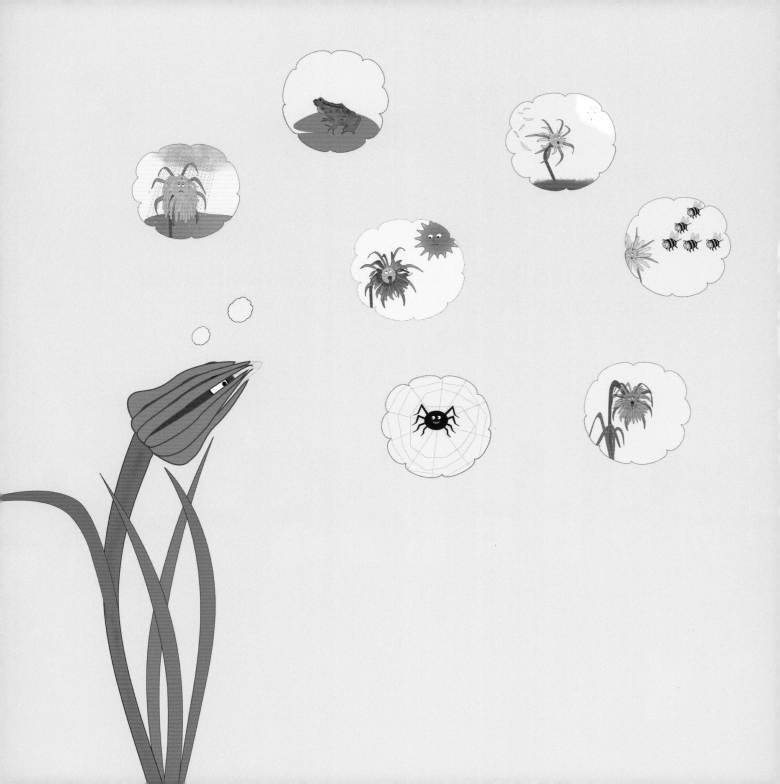

Tell Me

Why do you think the little bud was afraid?

What could you tell the little bud so that she'll no longer be afraid?

What did you learn from this book?

What did you already know?

Did you see?

The tortoise.

The bone.

The mouse running past the fence.

The kite.

The robin pecking at his seed.

The spider.

The frog.

The butterfly.

The goldfinch.

The mouse climbing out of the flower pot.

The hedgehog.

The owl.

The worm.

The rabbit.

About the Authors

Renée also writes and illustrates inspirational books - for adults - about self-reflection and the quirky traits of Humanity for those, who like her, question what they're doing in this world. She uses a character called Dilly to illustrate her points. Renée lives in Co. Leitrim in Ireland.

G R Hewitt was born in England and has lived and worked in France and Ireland for the last few years - he now lives in Ireland. Though it was not his job *per se*, his work required copy-writing, editing and designing skills but these were never as rewarding as writing and illustrating a more personal project. He enjoyed working on *The Frightened Little Flower Bud* and suspects more books may be in the pipeline.

Authors' Notes

Books are rather like parables - we understand them on one level when we first read them and others as time goes by. With this in mind, it's best not to try to 'explain' this book to children for they absorb far more from books than we give them credit for. To 'explain' it to them bypasses - and hinders - the development of their own wonderful imagination, replacing it with our own. It's best to let children get from this book what they're ready to get from it and to answer - as simply as possible - questions they might raise. For some it's just a story, and for others it goes deeper. So for example, if reading it to a 4 year old, it should be read as a book that's about the life-cycle of a flower and no more - some children will just enjoy the pictures. Older children may wish to discuss other aspects of this book that resonate in some way with them.

The questions at the back of this book were designed to stimulate the imagination and to encourage discussion. The 'Did You See?' page is a fun way to develop observational skills.